To:
_____

_____

Our pets teach us how to love and also how to mourn.
They show us that happiness can be found in the most simplest things.

The loss of a beloved pet can be devastating, but I've always found comfort in knowing that just like us, pets have a chance to go to a better place. A place filled with pure joy, unconditional love and an endless supply of yummy treats! I hope this book not only comforts your family in times of heartache, but also reaffirms the promise of God's steadfast love for us all...including our furry friends!

Melanie

Pets in Heaven by Melanie Salas
Published by Golden Crown Publishing, LLC

www.GoldenCrownPublishing.com

© 2021 Golden Crown Publishing, LLC

Created by Melanie Salas
ISBN:978-1-954648-56-2

Pets In Heaven

Created by
Melanie Salas

I know that God is taking great care of you

And it makes my heart happy that God is getting to love you too!

when I think
about
all the fun
we had.

In Heaven,
I bet there
are a million
places to run.

I know you are happy, l♥ved and having fun!

So,
even though
we had
to say
goodbye,

I will continue to look for you up in the sky.

And
I will know
as I see the
beautiful clouds
of white...

Or the shining stars at night...

that you
will always be
up there looking
at me...

watching me become all that I can be!